The Golden Goose

THE BROTHERS GRIMM

RETOLD AND WITH PICTURES BY *Uri Shulevitz*

FARRAR STRAUS GIROUX • NEW YORK

For P.S.B.

Library of Congress Cataloging-in-Publication Data. Shulevitz, Uri. The golden goose / the brothers Grimm ; retold and with pictures by Uri Shulevitz. — 1st ed.   p. cm. [1. Fairy tales. 2. Folklore—Germany.] I. Grimm, Jacob, 1785–1863. II. Grimm, Wilhelm, 1786–1859. III. Title. PZ8.S345154Go 1995 398.2'094302—dc20 [E] 94-44358 CIP AC

Once there was a father who had three sons, the youngest of whom was a simpleton.

One day the eldest son went to the forest to cut wood.
Before he left, his mother gave him a sweet cake.
In the forest he met an old man, who said, "I'm hungry.
May I have some of your cake?" The eldest son said, "If I
give you some, I won't have enough for myself."
When the son went to chop down a tree, he wounded
his arm.

The second son went to cut wood. Before he left, his mother gave him a sweet cake. In the forest he met the old man, who asked him for some of his cake. Like his brother, he refused. And when he went to chop down a tree, he wounded his leg.

Then the simpleton wanted to cut wood. His father said, "You'll only hurt yourself." But the simpleton begged so hard that at last he was allowed to go. Before he left, his mother gave him a piece of dry bread.

He met the old man, who asked him for some of his cake. The simpleton said, "I have only a piece of dry bread. If that pleases you, we will eat it together." But when he pulled out the bread, it was a sweet cake.

After they had eaten, the old man said, "Since you have a kind heart, I'll give you good luck. Cut down this tree and you will find it." And then he vanished.

When the simpleton cut down the tree, he found a goose
with feathers of pure gold.

He took the goose and went to an inn to stay the night.

The innkeeper had three daughters—
Anabelle, Clarabelle, and Loulabelle.
When they saw the goose, they each
had an irresistible desire to have a
golden feather.
As soon as the simpleton fell asleep,
Anabelle tiptoed into his room.

But the moment she touched the goose,

Hokety, pokety, stickety, stuck, poor Anabelle was down on her luck.

Wiggle and pull, she couldn't shake loose, and she had to stay with the simpleton's goose.

After a while, Clarabelle went up to see what was keeping her sister. As soon as she touched Anabelle,

Hokety, pokety, stickety, stuck, poor Clarabelle was down on her luck.
Wiggle and pull, she couldn't shake loose; she, too, had to stay with the simpleton's goose.
Finally, Loulabelle went to see why her sisters weren't coming down. "For
goodness' sake, help us!" they begged her. But when Loulabelle touched
Clarabelle,
Hokety, pokety, stickety, stuck, poor Loulabelle was down on her luck.
Wiggle and pull, she couldn't shake loose; she, too, had to stay with the simpleton's goose.
So they all had to spend the night there.

In the morning, the simpleton took the goose and left the inn. He didn't notice Anabelle, Clarabelle, and Loulabelle following him.

On the way, they met a parson. When the parson saw the girls, he cried out, "For shame, young ladies. It isn't proper to chase after a young fellow!" He tried to pull Loulabelle away, and,

Hokety, pokety, stickety, stuck, the poor parson was down on his luck.

Wiggle and pull, he couldn't shake loose; he, too, had to follow the simpleton's goose.

Soon they met the sexton. The sexton whispered to the parson, "Your reverence, what will people say when they see your reverence chasing after young ladies?" He touched the parson's sleeve, and,
Hokety, pokety, stickety, stuck, the poor sexton was down on his luck.
Wiggle and pull, he couldn't shake loose; he, too, had to follow the simpleton's goose.

In the fields, they met a peasant. The sexton called to the peasant, "Help
set us free!" But as soon as the peasant touched the sexton,
Hokety, pokety, stickety, stuck, the poor peasant was down on his luck.
Wiggle and pull, he couldn't shake loose; he, too, had to follow the simpleton's goose.

Farther down the road, they met the peasant's wife. When she saw her
husband running, she ran after him, and called to him to stop. When he
didn't stop, she took hold of his shirt, and,
Hokety, pokety, stickety, stuck, the poor peasant's wife was down on her luck.
Wiggle and pull, she couldn't shake loose; she, too, had to follow the simpleton's goose.

At last they came to a city.

It was ruled by a king whose only daughter was so serious that no one could make her laugh. This worried the king, so he had proclaimed that whoever could make her laugh would marry her.

Upon learning this, the simpleton ran straight to the royal palace.

When the guards tried to stop them,

Hokety, pokety, stickety, stuck, the poor royal guards were down on their luck.
Wiggle and pull, they couldn't shake loose; they, too, had to follow the simpleton's goose.

As soon as the princess saw the
parade, she burst into laughter, and
couldn't stop.

The simpleton claimed his bride. But the king didn't like
him for a son-in-law. So he tried to get out of his promise
and said, "Before you can have my daughter for a wife,
you must bring me a ship that sails on both water and
land."

The simpleton didn't know what to do, so he went to the forest to the spot where he had cut down the tree. And there was the old man.

The old man said, "Because you were kind to me, I will give you a ship that can sail on both water and land."
Now the king was forced to keep his promise.

The simpleton married the princess. And Anabelle,
Clarabelle, Loulabelle, the parson, the sexton, the
peasant, his wife, and the royal guards all danced at his
wedding.
He lived happily with his wife. And the golden goose
lived happily, too, and had many little golden geese, who
laid many golden eggs.